The Hug Store

by Shana and Rick Morrison

VLB Veronica Lane Books

Veronica Lane Books

www.veronicalanebooks.com email: etan@veronicalanebooks.com
2554 Lincoln Blvd. Ste 142, Los Angeles, CA 90291 USA
Tel: +1 (800) 651–1001

Cataloging–In–Publication Data
    Morrison, Rick 1966 –
    The Hug Store by Shana and Rick Morrison

Summary: A young girl learns the secret to finding the source of love and affection.

Audience: Ages 3–10

ISBN 978–16251777–1–1 (Hardbound)
ISBN 978–16251777–4–2 (Softbound)

This book of never-ending HUGS belongs to:

_____

More Hugs for our book...

Shana & Rick's creative and playful tale helps to enrichen a child's sense of love, self-worth and self-reliance. The importance of our common human need of embrace is a very useful concept to impart to children in our high tech, low touch society.

> – Dr. Diane Cirincione, PhD
> Founder, Attitudinal Healing
> Author, *Love Is The Answer* and
> *Change Your Mind, Change Your Life*

If you are looking for a book to connect emotionally with children *The Hug Store* is it! *The Hug Store* is a heartfelt story and beautifully depicts genuine self-awareness and emotional connection. *The Hug Store* is a wonderful addition to any child's library.

> – Jenna Laski, LMFT
> Parent Educator, Los Angeles CA

From Shana and Rick, Big Hugs to:

Tamar Andrews, Rickie Byars Beckwith, Michael Bernard Beckwith, Leslie Berlin, Etan Boritzer, Leigh Simran Brown, Leon Campbell Jr, Paul John Castro, Diane Cirincione, Dana Cooper, Jake Cooper, Noah Cooper, Jason Cooper, Howard Fridson, Tom Gorman, Sonal Goyal, Matt Hertenstein, Gerald Jampolsky, Sherry Kaufman, Nori Klar, Jenna Laski, Bob Lindquist, Suzi Lula, Julie Moret, Shana Morrison, Lisa Morrison, Diane Morrison, Herb Morrison, Beth Robinson, Carlos Santana, Ruta Sepetys, Goran Skakic, Diane Stevenson, Shefali Tsabary, Keiko Yabushita, Marcia Yashinsky, Jerry Yashinsky, Joel Yashinsky, Jeff Yashinsky, Warren Zide

The Hug Store

by Shana and Rick Morrison

Veronica Lane Books

This is Shana's family: Mommy, Daddy, Aunt Dana, Cousin Jake and Cousin Noah, Uncle Jason, Grandma and Grandpa.

Oh, and Shana's dog Baxter.

One Sunday, all of Shana's family are having lunch together at Grandma and Grandpa's home.

After lunch, Grandpa asks, "Would anybody like to help me pick up the leaves that fell from the trees?"

Shana raises her hand and says, "Grandpa, I want to help!"

"OK, Shana," Grandpa says, "Let's go!"

Grandpa and Shana pick up leaves for a long time.

When they finish, Grandpa says, "Shana thank you for helping me pick up all those pretty leaves. That was a big job and I'm so glad you were here to help!"

"I like to help you, Grandpa!" Shana says.

Grandpa says, "It is so nice to have you visiting us, Shana.
Grandma and I have missed you sooo much.
How about a big hug for Grandpa?"

Shana says, "Sorry Grandpa, I'm all out of hugs!
I have to go to the store to get some more hugs
and I will bring one home for you."

On Monday, Shana and Mommy are at the grocery store.

Shana asks, "Mommy, what aisle are the hugs on? I promised Grandpa that I would get him some hugs when we were at the store."

Mommy says, "Shana dear, this is a grocery store.
I don't think they sell hugs here. They only sell healthy
and delicious food here."

"Oh," says Shana, a little sad.

On Tuesday, Shana and Grandma are at an arts and crafts store. Shana asks, "Grandma, what aisle are the hugs on? I promised Grandpa I would get him some hugs when we went to the store."

s Arts & Crafts

Grandma says, "Shana sweetheart, this is an arts and crafts store. I don't think they sell hugs here. They only sell paint, stickers, crayons, and other stuff to help you create your beautiful art projects."

On Wednesday, Shana and Aunt Dana are at the shoe store.

Shana asks, "Aunt Dana, what aisle are the hugs on? I promised Grandpa that I would get him some hugs when we went to the store."

Aunt Dana says, "Shana this is a shoe store.
I don't think they sell hugs here.
They only sell shoes and socks, and stuff like that.
Look at all the pretty shoes everywhere Shana!
Which shoes do you like better, the pink ones
or the blue ones?"

Shana says, "The pink ones!"

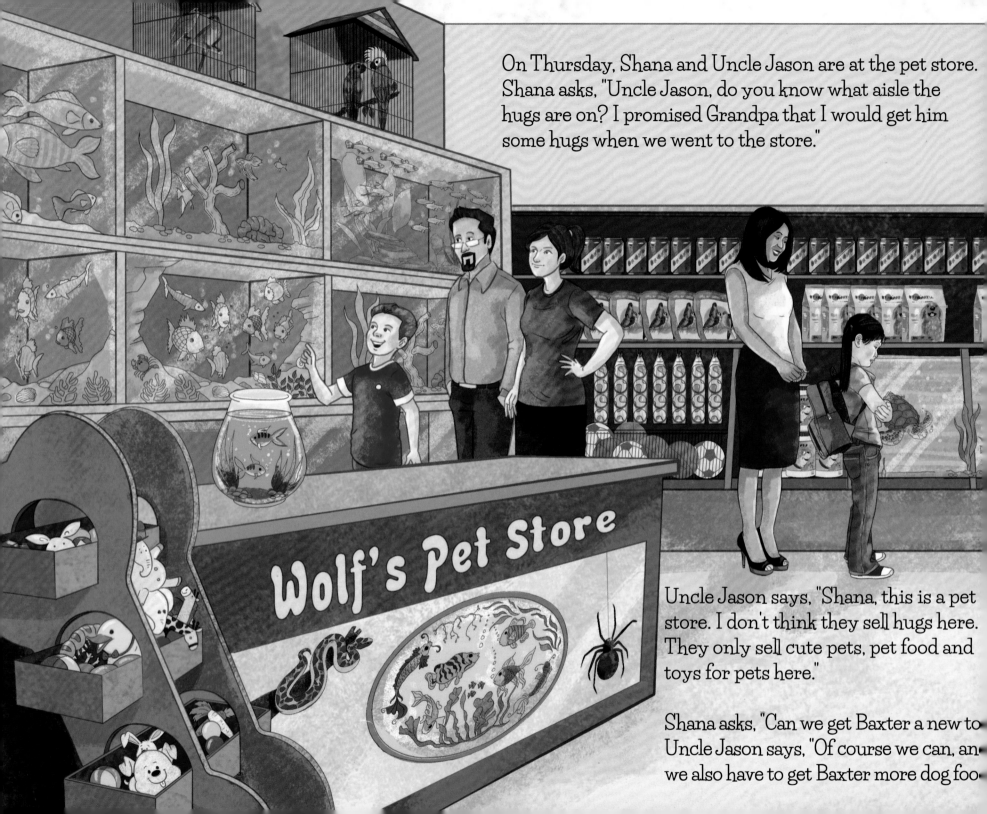

On Thursday, Shana and Uncle Jason are at the pet store. Shana asks, "Uncle Jason, do you know what aisle the hugs are on? I promised Grandpa that I would get him some hugs when we went to the store."

Uncle Jason says, "Shana, this is a pet store. I don't think they sell hugs here. They only sell cute pets, pet food and toys for pets here."

Shana asks, "Can we get Baxter a new to Uncle Jason says, "Of course we can, an we also have to get Baxter more dog foo

Tom's Terr

On Friday, Shana, and cousins
Jake and Noah are at the toy store.

Shana asks, "Jake and Noah, do you know what aisle
the hugs are on? I promised Grandpa that I would get
him some hugs when we went to the store."

Cousin Noah says, "Shana silly, this is a toy store.
They don't sell hugs here, only toys, and lots of them!
Look at them all!"

Shana asks, "Will you buy me that big pink ball up there? It's my favorite color!"

Cousin Jake says, "Yes we'll buy it, and take it home and play catch in the front yard,
now that you and Grandpa have cleaned up all the leaves."

On Saturday, Shana and Daddy are at the music store.

Shana asks, "Daddy, what aisle are the hugs on at this store? I promised Grandpa I would get him some hugs when we went to the store."

Daddy says, "Shana this is a music store. I don't think they sell hugs here. They only sell guitars, pianos and other instruments that make pretty musical sounds."

"But Daddy," Shana says almost in tears. "I've been to six stores this week looking for hugs. Where can I buy a hug for Grandpa?"

Daddy says, "Well Sweetheart, I don't know of any stores where you can buy hugs, but I know there is a hug store somewhere where you will discover as many hugs as you will ever want."

"Please take me to that hug store Daddy," Shana says.
Daddy smiles and says "Shana, I think you know where that hug store is..."
Shana thinks... and thinks... and thinks...

Suddenly a huge smile comes across Shana's face.

"Daddy!" Shana shouts out loud, "I figured it out!
I know where the hug store is! It's right here inside
my heart! I've been looking in the wrong place
all week. I am The Hug Store!"

Shana gives Daddy a huge hug and is really proud
of herself for finally realizing where the hug store is.

On Sunday, Shana, Mommy, Daddy, Aunt Dana, Cousin Jake, Cousin Noah, Uncle Jason, and Baxter all go back to Grandma and Grandpa's house for lunch.

When Shana walks in the door, she says to Grandpa,

"Grandpa I have something for you!"

"What's that, my precious?" Grandpa asks.

I have all the hugs in the world that you could ever want!

"Wow," Grandpa says, "Where did you find them, Shana?"

"I found them in the place where all the hugs in the world are!"

"Where are all the hugs in the world, Shana?" Grandpa asks.

"Right here, Grandpa!" Shana says, pointing to her heart! "How many would you like?" asks Shana.

"Can I have lots of hugs, Shana?" Grandpa asks.

"Sure," says Shana. "And don't worry Grandpa because The Hug Store never runs out of hugs!"

Shana starts to give Grandpa lots of hugs.

Shana finally found out where the real Hug Store is.

Do you know where your Hug Store is?

Benefits of Hugging

1) Reduces stress, worry and anxiety
2) Increases calmness
3) Reduces production of cortisol (the stress hormone)
4) Enhances bonding differently than language alone
5) Lowers levels of emotional and physical pain
6) Increases compassion & understanding
7) Relieves depression
8) Elevates mood
9) Boosts and enhances the immune system
10) Relaxes muscles in the body
11) Lowers blood pressure & improves heart health
12) Balances the nervous system
13) Reduces feelings of hostility and anger
14) Helps with non-verbal communication
15) Boosts self-esteem

F.A.Q.

What makes a good quality hug?

– A firm embrace that lasts 4–8 seconds. A firm hug stimulates the release of oxytocin, serotonin, and dopamine (the happy hormones). A flimsy hug won't hurt, but it won't help that much either.

How many hugs?

– Like both diet and exercise, you need a steady daily dose of hugging, at least 4–8 hugs per day.

When to hug?

– Morning, noon and night or anytime that feels right.

Who to hug?

– Anybody you want to and that you feel comfortable hugging. Group hugs are good too!

Is there a time when not to hug?

– Perhaps when sneezing!

From Rick,

It is my intention to educate children and adults about the wonderful benefits and joys of hugging. However, I would be remiss as a parent if I didn't further explore the idea of what constitutes safe hugging, and touching in general. For parents, teachers and childcare professionals, here are some suggested topics you can further discuss with children regarding safe hugging and touching.

– Who to hug? Who not to hug?

– Where to hug? Where not to hug?

– What is safe hugging?

– When to hug? When not to hug?

– When is a hug physically too hard or too rough?

– How long should you hug?

– What if somebody wants to do more than hug?

– Is hugging animals OK? Which ones yes, and which ones no?

About Rick and Shana...

Based upon a true story, The Hug Store idea was born during a family visit to Michigan that Shana and Rick took one Thanksgiving. When they arrived at Rick's parents' home, Grandpa (Rick's Father) asked Shana for a hug since he hadn't seen her in several months and missed her. Shana told Grandpa that she "was all out of hugs and needed to go to the store to get some more!"

Rick is a Realtor and previously enjoyed many years of sales and marketing in both the music business, as well as the wine business. Rick is a skilled musician and also enjoys all types of fitness activities, cooking, travel, arts and entertainment, charity work and self-development work.

Shana is 5 year old kindergartner who loves dogs, singing, dancing, karate, painting, magic tricks, chocolate, building forts, riding on top of her daddy's shoulders and of course, giving hugs! Shana lives in Los Angeles with her family.

Contact Info:

Rick Morrison/The Hug Store
10573 W. Pico Blvd #323
Los Angeles CA 90064
213-375-0917
thehugstore@gmail.com
www.TheHugStoreBook.com

Portion of sales proceeds from The Hug Store go to:

 National Center for Missing & Exploited Children

 The Touch Research Institute at the University of Miami School of Medicine.

www.TheHugStoreBook.com

Changing the world, one hug at a time...